This edition published by Parragon Books Ltd in 2013

Parragon Books Ltd
Chartist House
15–17 Trim Street
Bath BA1 1HA, UK
www.parragon.com

ISBN 978-1-4723-3196-0

Printed in China

MARVEL
SPIDER-MAN

PaRRagon

Bath • New York • Singapore • Hong Kong • Cologne • Delhi
Melbourne • Amsterdam • Johannesburg • Shenzhen

Peter Parker was a student at Midtown High. He enjoyed all his classes, but science was his favourite. He was the best student Midtown High had seen in many years and his teachers were very proud of him. The only thing Peter loved more than science was his family. He lived with his Aunt May and his Uncle Ben in Queens, New York.

One day, Peter went to the science hall for a demonstration. He couldn't wait to see how the scientists would control a radioactive wave!

The rays were ready. Peter eagerly looked on. He was thrilled to be there, in the company of such brilliant scientists.

Everyone was so fascinated with the demonstration
that no one noticed when something unplanned occurred.
A spider descended between the rays just as they were
activated. And as the radioactive spider fell, dying, it bit the
nearest living thing. Which happened to be Peter Parker.

As soon as he was bitten, Peter felt weak and tired. Peter just wanted to get out of the dark laboratory and into the fresh air. Peter felt a sudden, peculiar tingling in his head. It was an itching, urging, nagging feeling. The only thing he understood about it was that he was meant to react. To do something.

So he did.

Peter was sure he was dreaming.

He couldn't really be climbing up a wall. Nobody could do that.

When he reached the roof, he grabbed on to a chimney – and crushed it! He didn't have that kind of strength.

Peter felt the tingly feeling again. This time it gave him the urge to spring. And so he jumped from one tall roof to another. And when he wanted to go back down to the street, the same strange feeling told him the easiest way to get there was to climb down a clothesline.

Peter stared at himself in amazement. How could this be happening?

Then, Peter realized he had started feeling different right after being bitten by that spider in the lab. Somehow the experiment must have affected the dying creature. And when it bit Peter, it transferred its power to him!

As he wandered home, amazed and half-dazed, a sign outside an old wrestling theatre caught his eye. It would be the perfect way to test all of his newfound abilities.

Peter was ready to test his new powers on a brutish wrestler called Crusher Hogan. Peter wore a disguise so that no one would make fun of him if his plan didn't work. He'd been teased and taunted enough. When Peter challenged him, Crusher Hogan laughed. But Crusher soon found that he was very wrong to do so.

Peter was paid well for the victory. A man in the crowd even asked him if he'd want to be on TV. Things were going great. Plus, Peter had his Aunt May and Uncle Ben at home. His uncle had even saved up for a special microscope that Peter had wanted.

Uncle Ben reminded him that knowledge and science were power. "And," Uncle Ben told Peter, "with great power comes great responsibility."

Peter was too excited to settle down. He used his new microscope, his chemistry set and his knowledge of science to create a very special fluid. It had the strength and stickiness of a spider's silk. Then he created devices that could spin the fluid into a web the same way a spider would.

He called them his web-shooters. Finally, he designed a sleek new costume. Now all he needed was a stage name. He arrived at one as good as any other....

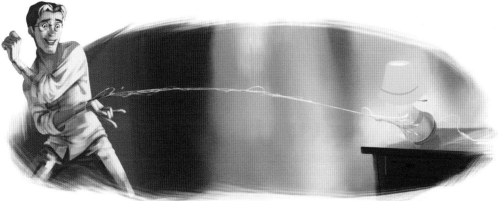

SPIDER-MAN!

Peter's TV appearances were a huge hit. After all, who wouldn't be amazed by a Spider-Man climbing up walls and swinging from his own webs.

Soon everyone wanted a piece of Spider-Man. Peter was starting to feel important, wanted ... and powerful! No one would ever be able to push him around again. Not when he had powers like these.

Peter got lost thinking about how wonderful his new life would be. He daydreamed about fame and celebrity. And when a security guard called for help down the studio hall, Peter ignored him.

The crook that the guard was chasing raced into a lift. The doors closed and the thief escaped.

But Peter didn't care. He had great power. And from now on, he only needed to look out for one person – himself.

It didn't take long for Peter to forget about the guard and the escaped criminal. In fact, by the time he got home they were the furthest things from his mind. He was just happy to be with the people who loved him. And in his spare time, when he was not studying or home with his family, Peter went out as the famous, spectacular Spider-Man!

But one night on his way home from a TV performance, Peter arrived to find something worrisome. Peter knew something was terribly wrong – and he was right. His Uncle Ben had been killed by a criminal. The police officers told Peter not to worry. They had the crook cornered at an old waterfront warehouse.

Peter ran upstairs, put on his costume ...

... and swooped over the city to avenge his uncle. Peter was quicker and more furious than ever before.

At last, Peter arrived at the warehouse.
He landed on the far wall.

The thief was stunned.
And that's when Spider-Man sprung into action!

The crook's hat flew from his head and Peter finally took a good look at him. Peter felt a heavy weight in his chest. It couldn't be. But it was.

The man who had killed his uncle was the same
man he allowed to escape into the lift at the
studio. If only Peter had stopped him then!
If only he had not acted so selfishly!

Stunned, Peter tied up the criminal in webbing and dangled him off a streetlamp for the police to find. The most Peter could do now was prevent him from hurting anyone else. Through the haze of his grief, Peter realized it was not about money or fame or any of the other rewards his power could give him.

He had finally realized that what his Uncle Ben had told him was true: with great power comes great responsibility. And that was the rule that Peter Parker lived by from that day forwards.